Weatl

MW01178907

Contents

written by Pam Holden

Weather impacts on our everyday life in lots of ways, influencing
the choices we make about what we will do and where we will
go, as well as basic things such as which clothes we should wear,
and what food we'll eat. Weather can even impact on how you
feel physically (hot or cold), and emotionally (happy or sad).

Extreme weather can affect your life in important ways, such as your safety in a severe storm or flood. Make sure there are emergency plans in place with your family and school, so that everyone will know where to seek shelter during severe weather. Prepare a survival kit with enough supplies to last several days. Follow newspaper, radio and television weather reports giving warnings.

Weather scientists called meteorologists study all types of weather, so that they can forecast the weather for several days ahead. They observe conditions of the atmosphere such as temperature, wind, rain and clouds, using weather satellites to take pictures of weather formations. The information they collect can be reported to predict what weather is coming; their reports help people to prepare for the impact of the weather on their activities; warning messages make people aware of trouble ahead.

Weather reports are needed by people who work outdoors, where rain, snow, wind, thunder and lightning can impact on their plans: e.g. Farmers need suitable weather to plant or harvest crops, and to take care of their animals. Others affected are builders, gardeners, cyclists and hikers. Sometimes sports events and special occasions have to be cancelled. Warnings of coming storms help people take shelter and protect their property. Fishermen stay away from the sea, pilots don't fly, drivers avoid dangerous roads, and families stay indoors.

There are many different kinds of weather in the world – the coldest areas have snow, ice, hail, and icy wind, while warmest regions have sunshine, droughts and breezes. These differences impact on many parts of life: e.g. the type of housing varies from cool houses with open shady decks to cosy homes with heating. Clothes worn in warm weather are a few light garments, open shoes and shady hats; layers of warm clothes are needed in cold weather, with shoes, socks, cosy hats and gloves. Sports and leisure activities in summer include swimming, boating, hiking, cycling, barbecues and picnics, while winter suits skiing, skating, ball games, etc. Transport in warm weather can include bicycles, boats and open cars, which are unsuitable in cold conditions.

Wind blows air
from place to place,
sometimes taking
the rain away, but it
often has bad effects.
A small fire can be
fanned by strong
winds, growing to a
wildfire that spreads
through dry forests
destroying homes,
farms, and taking
lives. Wild winds
sometimes cause
disasters at sea, when
boats are tipped over
and ships blown onto
rocks.

ROAD CLOSED

Rain is needed to provide life-giving water, but too much rainfall can cause flooding that impacts badly on people as their homes are ruined; crops that are relied on for food are destroyed; animals are drowned on flooded farmland; roads, bridges and railways are damaged and unusable. Landslides and flashfloods happen suddenly, leaving people stranded or injured.

When there is plenty of sunshine, but not enough rain, the result is a drought – waterways like rivers and streams dry up, the land becomes dry and dusty, crops and gardens don't grow, and animals suffer.

In cold parts of the world, snow and ice bring great fun with sports using skis, skates and sleds, but there are problems with heavy snowfalls blocking roads and slippery ice causing accidents. Schools are closed and adults can't get to work. Animals starve when they cannot reach food that is buried under snow, and crops are spoiled by sudden frosts and snowfalls.

Shelter is needed from the impact of all kinds of extreme weather – storms or the heat of the sun. Thunder and lightning are frightening and dangerous. Find shelter as soon as you see lightning or hear thunder. If you can't get inside a safe building, a closed vehicle can provide protection from lightning. Stay well away from trees!

Rescue services are needed wherever the weather has a bad impact causing an emergency. People in danger need expert help quickly. In some situations a change to better weather has a good effect: floods wash away, snow and ice melt, bushfires are put out, seas calm down, sailors are rescued, landslides are cleared, and rain falls on crops.

Weather will always affect our everyday life.